In the Well

In the Well

by Elizabeth Tibbetts

Winner of the 2002 Bluestem Poetry Award

Bluestem Press
Department of English
Emporia State University
Emporia, Kansas

Printed in Canada

Library of Congress Cataloging-in-Publication Data

Tibbetts, Elizabeth, 1953-
 In the well / by Elizabeth Tibbetts
   p. cm.
 ISBN 1-878325-26-4 (alk. paper) — ISBN 1-878325-27-2 (pbk. :
alk. paper)
 I. Title.

 PS3620.I23I5 2003
 813'.6—dc21
                        2003041838

Acknowledgments

Grateful acknowledgment to the following publications where some of these poems have appeared, sometimes in slightly different form.

The American Scholar: "Madonnas"
The Beloit Poetry Journal: "A Nurse Reads *A Book of Luminous Things*," "Fertility," "Ida Goes to the Hens," "In the Well," "Institution"
The Cafe Review: "An Invitation," "Kissing the Sky"
Calyx: "Climbing Grief," "Eighty-Five," "Full as Pie," "She Steps Closer," "When Lavender Comes"
Green Mountains Review: "Change in View," "Coming Home," "My Brother and I," "Women and Hens: Postcard—Mozambique"
Icarus: "Mission San Xavier Del Bac"
The Laurel Review: "The Strip"
The Maine Progressive: "Black Ice"
Maine Times: "Snow"
Prairie Schooner: "Book of Weeks," "The Muse Visits After I'll Never Write Another Chicken Poem"
Puckerbrush Review: "From the Hemlocks," "The Island" "October," "Kissing the Sky," "The Waiting," "With Flowers"
Rivendell: "In the Lingerie Store"
The Spoon River Poetry Review: "Home Visit"
West Branch: "After a Dark Winter," "Perfect Selves"

"Black Ice" also appeared in *The Art of Maine in Winter* (Down East Books, 2002).
Some poems from this book appeared in the chapbook *Perfect Selves* (Oyster River Press, 2001).

I am deeply grateful to all the people who sustained me through completion of this book, including Kate Barnes, Barb Cameron, Kristen Lindquist, Betsy Sholl, Marion Stocking, Candice Stover, my mother and father, Zachary and Aileen, and my beloved Jim.

Thank you to Blue Mountain Center and the Ragdale Foundation where I was given time and space to write some of these poems. Special thanks to Bluestem Press and Elizabeth Dodd.

For my mother and father and Kate Barnes, with love

Contents

III

IV

In the Well

There was a trout,
said the old woman who lived here,
if I can believe the one who called me
always by the wrong name, who accused
me of stealing her blind—she could still see
that I had what once was hers.
                                    Once, she was
a young woman whose man lowered a shining trout
in a bucket into the well he had dug, digging
his body deeper until she saw only brow
and then no man at all. She dreamed
of the fish circling underground, feeding
on lost insects and worms, while snakes coiled
between the cold stones above the water's surface.
The fish dreamed of other fins and tails
and pale, speckled bellies. And when the fish saw
that the woman lifted the cover and poured in the sun,
did it believe she would jump, her descent
and splash slowed by its joy at her approaching
toes, her moon-colored thighs,
the drifting skirt, her hair streaming up
like pickerel grass, bubbles of light
rising around her as if she carried the sky
down to live in the watery dark, emitting gold
and green and blue?
                                    There was a woman, a fish,
and a man whose hands placed the stones
where a face looks up now from that plate of sky.

I

Woman and Hens: Postcard—Mozambique

Look at this woman smoking a pipe
and bearing two bound hens on her head,
the blue pillow they sit on, the woman's
red and green striped shirt. The hens
are craning their necks, heads jerking
side to side, red eyes hungry
for the passing fields and road.

They are the blossoms on a woman's head.
They are the jewels in her crown. They are
hens of the highest order.

Perhaps she's hurrying home to her husband
and other wives, or to a dying child.
Maybe she's humming time to her feet,
modeling that hat for a buck or two,
or she's just hungry for the good soup
she'll cook after she lops the hens' heads
off and their bodies run until life
runs out of them and they are gutted,
plucked, and dropped into the pot.

All we know is the look
of hens that are riding high
before whatever happens happens

Change in View

Rich in God, I'd walked home,
not expecting my uncle's long, black car,
or his hound bounding onto me.
Flat on my back beneath the dog

I saw loose ears, balls and jowls,
and a sun-lit puzzle of elm branches,
fully leafed, and blue Sunday-sky.
Fear didn't hold me there;

it was the sudden change in view
and all my senses snapping open
so that the unyielding ground seemed
like something I could never leave,

nor the dog's frank scent,
nor our syncopated breathing,
until the front door scraped open
and my mother's voice slapped

the dog off me. I ran inside
and kissed Uncle Albert who sat
behind tight suspenders and held
a fat cigar like a smoking prize.

Beside him, as bright as a window,
Aunt Winnie with gorgeous lips
posed inside the blue haze,
and her long fingers beckoned me

to her scented lap as though she'd not
be dead in a month, rouged
but inert in a casket, and my own fingers
wouldn't start from her cold, pink hand,

and the ground would not break,
shovels wouldn't cut its shadowed face.

Madonnas

Fair Mary, caught mid-task (one hand raised
to fend off the kneeling angel's words),
your face is stilled by news you never
expected. How dare a mortal compare
herself to you?   And yet is this
what the painter asked for: the dimension
of understanding, the heart yearning
toward his canvas, the small hairs
of the arms rising in response
to your expression?

*

In my painting the word
arrives by phone. At the end
of a bleached hallway, Mary
is standing and holds the receiver
near her ear—words visible
in that few inches of air—
as she listens to the stranger
telling her news that changes
everything.

*

Here, from inside her gilded frame,
Mary stares beyond us. The baby
in her arms holds a pomegranate,
and seems to need a nap. Maybe
Mary needs one too, Jesus being
old enough to toddle into plenty
of trouble. Maybe she hasn't slept
for days, but she looks as though
she knows what's most unbearable,
and wonders how any god
could do this to a woman and child.

*

My friend's five-year old likes the devil
with bodies squirming in his mouth,
and the round painting of Mary
(standing on cherubs' heads)
holding young Jesus, who holds
a valentine wrapped in thorns.
He wants to know why the heart
is outside the body and wrapped in wire.

*

And was there a painting of a girl
rising from a chair by the heater
in a small kitchen? Perhaps
a red-checked cloth on the table,
a wall-lamp for purposes of light
and shadow. Her belly a melon
beneath her gown. Maybe two
paintings. One of her hearing
the sound of boots on the stairs.
The other showing an open door,
light striking a man's face—his hair
still hidden in the dark entry—
and his bare hand lit, too, holding out
a red deer heart for her.

*

And here, what this girl in the mirror
is holding onto is—what?
The baby boy on her hip and a bit
of vanity? They look good. Beyond her
is the landscape of her former life,

a room of books and a window
that looks out to the neighbors'
pear tree, which is just past bloom
and now setting tiny fruit. The girl
looks and looks. If she could just
stay here, like this, in glass,
some things might turn out all right.

Oranges

The moon rose as bold as an orange out of the bay
that night. It was nothing you said, it wasn't
your hand sneaking up my thigh that convinced me,
as I fiddled with the radio, its tiny green light
licking along the dial. Who can say what sends us
here, I mean here, now.
                                 All I can imagine is that fate
makes us what we are, or, with a sudden shift of cells,
a crack appears, fine as a hair, and we slip through,
the past grabbing our asses. Maybe I was caught
by a bone-deep radio voice traveling the sky—
who can say—but something pushed me the night
I stared into your eyes and straddled your lap
with the bony steering wheel at my back.

I've always wondered if I knew then what I was after,
or how I'd break away, years later, your scent on me,
the way an orange lingers on your fingers, its oils
mixing with the skin's, long after the fruit
has disappeared section by section.

Talking to God

The rooster is talking to God.
He says, "My mistress is afraid of the darkness
that holds her in one hand in the morning
and tosses her into the other hand in the afternoon.

When she brings water I tell her, look,
the oak leaves are the color of russet potatoes,
the sugar maples shine like my old Brahma hen
who is eggless but carries all my gold."

With Flowers

1
　　　　　　I had a dark-haired friend
as a child. We went out her back gate, latched it,
and ran into the field where blackberries' arched canes
bore to the ground. We lay down. Wind and sun
moved our flat, naked bodies and we took turns tickling
with long stems. When her mother called we dressed fast
and ran back laughing, pulling grass from our hair.
Then her father caught us, his quiet words cutting us
away from our skins. After that we stayed home,
buried our bare feet in the cool sandbox and cooked
cakes that we molded in buckets and covered with wild
vetch, daisies, clover, and ferns.

2
　　　　　　　At the student exhibit
in the Museum School a man in a sandbox won
two thousand dollars after he sat with his prosthesis
and trickled grains over his bare-stump-remnant of thigh.
Above him one hundred and forty-four photographs of his face
hung on the white museum wall. Other fake legs and canes
scattered the floor among dark, dry roses. No hint
of the land mine that turned his leg into a scarred loaf.
I didn't know where to look. Was he looking for more
than a prize, for some sharing, a woman to open her blouse
and show her empty chest?

3
　　　　　　A young woman from the island came in
to have her breast removed, her left. She was surprised,
but didn't cry, question, or scream in her sleep, at least
not there. She looked at the flaming incision, its bristling
stitches, and tucked a sock in her bra when she went home.
Two years later she came back, got a bouquet of carnations,
and lost a kidney, a piece of liver, and a section of ribs.
I checked her dressings, then went into a bathroom, locked
the door, and touched myself: breasts, chest, belly,
hips and thighs.

My Brother and I

Mother shut us in the corner
cupboard beneath the counter
where she kneaded bread and
rolled crust. We begged for this,
and fit neatly, our chins tucked
to our chests beside the big
yellow flour tin. We filled
the space perfectly like twins
waiting in the dark to be born.
When she left to answer the phone
we heard water boiling,
the clock ticking and her voice
as far away as another life.

Cowboys

When Brenda calls for the first time in thirty years
and mentions Cindy, I can't remember the Indian girl
who lived down the street—then her face
floats up through time like a dead child's in the sea,

and I tighten for the punch of words to tell me
some creep has cut and disassembled the woman
who used to be that thin, brown girl. But it's a different
story: the three of us played robbers, my fake gold

disappeared, and I insisted Cindy took it.
It was Bendra. She's been carrying this confession,
now lays down this scrap of our past as a Christian act,
so it's my turn to bear it, though I can't remember that day.

All I recall is the summer night Cindy's mother
banged at our door. She was crying—her mouth lipsticked,
whiskey on her breath—wailing for her lost daughter
who must have fallen off the docks, screeching for her girl

who couldn't swim. The neighbor men went out.
There were voices and lights; late into the night her name
traveled the street, rocked on our porch, and climbed
through my bedroom window, until hours later

the shout went up—she was alive, hiding on the beach.
Though I knew they'd found her, all that long night
I saw minnows nibbling her fingers, seaweed lifting
on the piers, and her black hair waving with it.

Prayers

After a childhood of loving God and his rituals,
I left the church at sixteen when animosity rose
inside me and I wanted to knock the women's hats off.
I'd been a girl who sang *Kyrie* from her feet,
who loved walking the long burgundy aisle to receive
the body of Christ and the biggest sip of his grape
Manischevitz blood she could manage. So

coming into church alone, after a two-decade lapse,
I expect something to happen. The windows
still tell the old stories—love and birth, murder
and miracles—but Jesus does not come down
to embrace me with that old, cozy feeling. It's cold,

and God has a parable of a girl he knew, young, big
with baby, who opened his heavy doors. She'd walked
dark miles past woods and snowy fields, sat
and watched the candle flickering above the altar,
then walked back home to a man who kneeled
in the living room, still polishing his new,
yellow Yamaha 650 motorcycle. And then—

but three women, ignoring God, begin to talk in back,
their words rending the story like thorns on stockings,
so I can't hear what happened next—his point.
When I stalk past them I see they're the women
(no longer in hats) I used to dream when I was four,
old ladies who waited their turn a long time, while I sat,
dressed in lace and patent leather shoes, on Jesus' lap,
and ran my fingers through the bright waterfall of his beard.

In the Beginning

In the beginning when the boy
was a new baby, and fussy evenings,
she tucked him into his basket

beneath the long, slanted rear window
of his father's silver Barracuda
and they'd all go driving under pink

and pigeon-colored skies. Back then
she didn't worry about crashing—
glass cascading onto his fresh face—

but imagined sunsets streaking
above him. Sometimes they just drove
around and around town, but other times

they parked above the beach and let
the motor idle. The baby stirred
as he slipped into sleep, his hands

curled, his lips sucking as he dreamed
his way down to his mother's arms.
The mother and father were quiet

as they looked out to where clouds
blazed and deepened and repeated
themselves on the puckered bay.

When Lavender Comes

It may fall like a blow to the cheek
or appear with blue in shadows
beneath the eyes of a child,
its tired mother, and the dying.

Or, if you're lucky,
it may rush you in lilacs
with their heavy-breasted blossoms,
or slip through the evening sky,

or rise in your mother's cotton apron
filled with tiny white stars as if,
with this tied around her,
she could fly.

An Invitation

It is a March day, the ground spongy
with melted snow. Newly returned grackles
spark purple and green as they startle
from the lawn. The dead are calling,

"Dress yourself," as if it were as simple
as unpinning a shirt from the line to wear
cloth cooler than skin, and the sun
like a hand on your hair.

Enormous maple limbs lie on the ground,
brought down by a storm that iced every twig.
Now the trunks trickle sap into buckets
and boughs wait to be burned

while gray squirrels write across the lawn
in cursive bounds; *mmm* they spell
with their curved backs and tails. All winter
they have hung upside down at the feeder,
ignoring the hand knocking on the glass.

The young poet who drowned, weighted by rocks,
has thawed and breathes again. Ice rotten,
the lake is an invitation, wide arms of blue water.
She wrote, once, that skin is a window that can be opened.

Any Color You Please

Winnie, with your painted lips,
I can still see you: yellow hair waves
against your face, flowered silk
flows down you like spring water

over stones. You ascend night clouds,
toss a kiss my way like blowing
smoke from your fingers, and I try
to catch it, but I can't, and I can't

reach even your pale, fine ankles,
or those hole-in-the-toe shoes
where red nails peek through. So I
tie you to the sky and sleep with you

flying above my pillow. I was five
when you, my father's sister, half
sister—always only half—died
in the street, struck by a hit and run

drunk. Tits, ass, and eyes like a cat,
they buried you deep in the ground;
then told stories: how you tipped
too many cocktails down that throat,

stayed out until all hours, smoked,
burped, swore, and never broke Uncle
of wanting more, even when you were
bad. I never heard about your life

as a girl, only that you stamped
your feet and screeched until your howl
became that late night laugh. I heard
I was not to turn out like you. But God,

I love the color red. I loved the sight
of you, big female fire engine tearing up
the street. Sirens screaming. Bells and
glitter. Men hanging on. Burning eyes.

Winnie, if you were still here, now
eighty-five, I'd love even your worn-out
face, your slowed down, slangy ways.
I'd wash your feet and polish your nails

Heart's Flame, Copper Creme, Rave—
any color you please, just to feel
your hand in my hair and show you
my new embroidered, high-heeled shoes.

Stealing

First, I stared through the keyhole at the bed's
mountain of my mother's crooked knees,
ate all my brother's chocolate-covered cherries,
took a nickel from the Lenten box
when a nickel could save another child's life,

then burst out with bouts of honesty,
stripped the new doll at my party
so that the grandmother I didn't like
yanked her away, hauled me from the table,

and instructed Dad to give me no cake.
(But he did.) I told God I hated him, then said
the devil was talking, but I was sorry.
I rescued stunned birds from the road. So it went,
for every black mark there were more stars,

until, in the concrete First National store,
I stuffed a pack of Winstons into my jacket pocket:
Halloween (exactly four years
before the night I'd appear back home and carve
my parents' hearts with the curve of my belly).

But first my best friend and I walked the dark streets,
watched costumed kids blow door to door,
and smoked, smoke burning so deep it seemed
our airways became visible fireworks behind our ribs,
while the lit cigarettes led us like tiny lamps.

Now I'd tell any kid, "Don't," but back then
I had to tear myself away, march my body
through the gates and not look back,

let that small fire eventually lead
a sperm to find its way to an egg
inside me. Much the same way kids
mocked that milk leads a body to smack—
though milk never took *me* that far.

After my son was born, I wore, with pleasure,
a turquoise bikini and popcorn sweater that a boyfriend
pulled out like birds from beneath his jacket.

In a teak house where I cleaned each week,
polishing sterling tea sets and a Steinway grand,
I hurried through mopping, then stole time
at the piano to play, climbing each note like stairs.

I slept with a few I shouldn't have, and once
kept ten dollars that a gas station attendant
mistakenly gave me with change, the bill
sitting on my gloved palm as unexpected
as answered prayer or a finch landing there to feed.

Book of Weeks

It came today—an invitation to Jake's New York show,
a postcard of a lizard-green ceramic gun,
his "suicide-assassin pistol" sculpted with opposing
barrels, designed so that if you were to shoot a lover,
you'd shoot yourself. I had a friend

who used to leave her husband and three boys home,
pack a child's black plastic pistol in her purse, fly south,
and ride the New York subways alone at night,
touching up her wide lips in a compact mirror
just before the stop where she'd meet her lover, Angel,

who knew only the glossy woman who stepped out.
Lonely, I took the card inside, then went out to the garden
where the tulips had aged and softened—their red petals
splayed to show the dark stars of their hearts,
the pistils burning like candles, and the stamens

circling in their black pollen hoods. At least Angel
knew the shapes of their time together, the slim chapters
of Saturday and Sunday in the book of weeks.
But what did I know about Jake—who I couldn't have—
his eyes on me as our brief month fell away day by day?

Angel knew buildings' block shadows, the angles of dim stairs,
a thin slice of light triangulating as they opened
his door, the circles of dinner plates and her open mouth,
table and chair legs, her legs, and the changing,
grasping forms of their bodies locking and unlocking.

Perhaps he knew that what we see is not really there—
like what I saw (which is what I *meant* to tell you)
when I went out to check the mail: a red dog
loping along the roadside that turned back
to look at me with a fox's masked face—but maybe

Angel grabbed what was most true, before
it turned to dust, those moments with a woman
illuminated by streetlight who was brave enough
to lie for what she had to have, to believe
that even a toy gun could save her life.

Institution

The woman in too many clothes
with a mound of butts beside her as orderly
and small as a doll's woodpile? She's the woman
with changing voices: lawyer, whore, born-again,
and crazy—about baking. She doesn't think
of the cellar, its earth smell rising,
dusty jars of peaches, their gold hidden,
or the door with no inside latch. When she tries
her mind scatters like flocks of birds.

Or the woman kneeling in the dirt,
her skirt perfectly tucked around her knees,
and her pale, tentative hands in zinnias
and tomatoes. She's smiling (her lips
do this same trick in sleep) as if she were
never burned and broken into by an uncle
who, when he was with her among other people,
looked at her and lit matches. She has learned
to kneel for hours, steadying her hands on green
stalks. She has learned these are her hands
beneath the gauzy absence she'd wrapped
herself in. They are becoming as near and real
as the maple leaves that shadow her.

That woman in the hot pink dress, pacing
with her face in her palms, won't look up.
If she does, you'll be looking down
two dark holes where silent bullets wait.
She says it's like looking through cracked
glass, no edges align. She says the world's
a conspiracy, and if she lets go
of her head, she'll disappear.
You'd never believe by her fingers'
slimness and pearly, curving nails
that anyone could break them in a vise,
one by one, but beneath the skin
her bones remember.

If it weren't for these eyes and hands
this could be all flowers and birds.
You'd be willing to believe
that bees are singing tiny ballads
in your ears, but you're hearing words,
"loony, insane," and who could blame you
for believing this is not your garden?
Or you could look at it as beautiful,
the way the psyche wraps itself and hides
or breaks apart to survive, the way
a starfish grows from the lost arm of itself,
or the way a bulb divides, how life goes on
far from where we start, or how you, too,
could forget what you've lost.

Perfect Selves

The harbor was full of sewage
and occasional rubbers floating
like clear jelly fish, so we swam
at Salzedo's Beach in a clean

pocket of bay, where I clung
to my mother's bottom and back,
then learned to paddle beside her,
her long legs opening and closing,

arms drawing apart, and one hip
and shoulder skimming the surface.
I loved her body and the white linen trim
that separated the suit's black fabric

from her skin. Once, after we floated,
rocking in the swell, she said we were
happiest, our most perfect selves,
in water, because we came from water,

and I imagined myself, shrimp-sized,
flipping inside my mother's salty pool,
her inside Gram's, and Gram inside
her mother's, until I lost myself—the way

I disappeared staring at the Big Dipper,
the universe too immense for one small life—
and I ran out of the ocean, its floor
wild with kelp and blue, gaping mussels,

starfish and side-walking crabs, ran
from the possibility of ever leaving,
and slapped myself down on a flat rock
to sizzle like a smelt in the pan.

The Finish

When this linen meets your skin,
and your arms enter the embrace of sleeves,
you wear my fingers' touches:
old buttons, French seams. In the finish
of fine pleats and stitches
I become the one you long for—
mender of wounds—mountains
you could lose yourself in,
a woman with ears like shells
that listen to the bottom of the sea.

When I step out of my dress in the dark,
can you see the crossed eyes
I had as a child, my scarred knees,
or the dream devil's black and hungry
stare? With feathers at my back, or fire,
I trail my childhood in tatters
before you. The stitches you wear
are tiny and straight. Do you see
how the fabric around me tears,
how I am forever pinning and basting?

Dis-ease

A woman sits in the kitchen soaking her feet,
her skirt pulled to her knees, and sees the design
blood leaves as bruises. Still, she's an instrument
for life. She's aching, but has become well trained,
and is grateful now for the embrace of water
that soothes the small bones like a mother's arms.

In the hospital, after X-rays and probes, she was armed
for the news that she's dying, already two feet
in the grave. She only asked that the nurse water
the flowers on the sill, wishing she were designed
to recover that easily. Now her life is a train
hurtling forward, her bone marrow a broken instrument.

She knows the irony: that leukocytes are instrumental
for fighting disease, but hers have taken up arms
against her, and like religious zealots have trained
to crowd and kill. Already she's dizzy on her feet,
sometimes seeing flashes that remind her of the design
that sunlight flicks onto summer leaves or moving water.

If dying could be like entering a body of water,
she would gladly go, giving in the way an instrument
gives itself to music, its physical beauty designed
to express the soul. She would open her arms
to the ocean and stroke, kicking her tired feet
and swim to the deep water she's been training

for all her life. There are still days when the train
stops, and she's at the sink filling a glass with water,
and the floor squeaks as she shifts on her feet,
and the mantle clock is just an ordinary instrument,
with its hands that look more like arms,
not a menace with its time-ravaging design—

days when she can't comprehend mortality's design
that will make her lose everything, even her train
of thought—past and present falling from her arms,
her appetite gone, her mouth unable to water
for any meal, her brain a floundering instrument
that can no longer direct her hands or her feet.

The woman dries her feet, admiring their design,
how they're delicate instruments she's cared for and trained.
She rises from her armchair and lifts the bucket of water.

From the Hemlocks

From the hemlocks the guinea fowl screech.
Their un-oiled and rhythmic cries,
twins in sound to the old pump, pull
memory like water from the ground.
My small hands on the iron handle,
I work with all my girl might
while my brother holds his bold face
under a rush of water. Then I hold mine
in water, cold as plunging into the ocean.

The shining pail rocks between us
soaking our sneakers and socks
as we walk back to the camp
where sun has broken
through fog and spruce to dazzle
Ma's face and hair and our one
beautiful white hen
who runs to us in half-flight.

Full as Pie

In the bag on my back—where I carry
my words which are hissing and snapping
to get out, where I've hoarded a silk dress,
blue and changing as water,
and the moon I've run away beneath,
once or twice, that circles, in the small dark,
its delicious slices, until it rises as full as pie—
there's also a daughter with heron's legs
and ten tiny moons on her nails.
In the beginning, I barely knew she was there
until this girl began grabbing my words
in fat hands, biting them with first teeth.
Now— when I reach in and feel her hair,
and it's as thick as my kitchen broom,
or I see someone she might be
on the street with her leggy stalking,
and down still on her cheek that hints
of when she lay curled and quiet as a peach—
I'm wondering how there is room.
I've tried enticing her into silence with acorns,
with frogs and toads, whistle of the oriole,
but she's talking back now. I've threatened
with rocks and sticks, but she won't
shut up; she has a big mouth ready to eat
the world and speak it back to me.

Home Visit

I didn't want to be
where a ninety-year old woman
rocked and looked out
on purple finches
at the feeder while bruises
slipped into sight from her sleeves:

the handling a gift from her son
who was gun-loving and volatile
as gasoline. Surely, he didn't learn
this from her, whose one remaining
joy was riding miles in the car,

the back of her boy's head before her,
and the fields and trees of her whole life
streaming by her window. When did
his fury begin? When she bore him, one leg
too short, or two hundred years before?

Now she cried every day and he said
it drove him crazy. The only quiet ones
were the skinny tom that urinated
from room to room and the son's wife
who lay with her ruined back on the sofa

beneath the many eyes of Jesus Christ
looking out from all walls, clouds,
The Last Supper, and the cross.
I didn't want to tell them that no one
would come back to bathe

the old woman because of the gun,
and when I did, the son threw himself
to his feet, grabbed the rifle as if
by the hair, pointed it straight at me
a yard from my face, and screamed,

as he snapped the chamber open
to show it was empty, that there
was not a Godblasted thing to be afraid of.

45

In the Palm

In the waiting room, beside a collage of baby pictures,
the microsurgeon's wife, smart in navy and white,
discusses insurance and payment with my friend,
then tells how her husband holds his patients' hands
as they go under. As much as it's for comfort,

she's sure he's checking nailbeds and watching
monitors. We all know some patients never rise again.
The surgeon appears: fastidious, hair clipped close,
nails and glasses clean, the kind of man
you'd allow to cut you open, then sew you up.

An iron pig stands upright on his desk and proffers
business cards. Thick traffic honks and hums
five stories down on Longwood Avenue. We've driven
four hours, my friend longing for a child, seeking
relief. And *I've* been here before, hearing

the doctor's soft, Southern drawl. I want it again:
I want to curl into the palm of his hand, and I want
to be incised and stitched, and for one long night,
to be rocked in Dilaudid's arms: twelve euphoric hours
of imagining that someday an egg will make

its way in the dark and bump into a tired sperm.

Fertility

Out of my vagina came a dog—
a puppy, actually. It was Mothers' Day.
The black nose arrived and the body
followed out onto this path of mortality.
I watched the nurse clean her off
and admire her spots and tail. "But, I wanted
a girl," I said as I lay back and kneaded
my slack stomach, that empty sack.

In the night, while the pup lay swaddled
asleep in the nursery with the nurses'
low voices and laughter,
I woke up to a hen pecking at my breast,
her feathers as white as the moon
in my darkened room. "Where is she?"
I called. The startled hen,
with a flurry of clucks and dusty feathers,
flew out my open window to the owls.
My breasts, full for twenty years,
let down their silent streams.

In Exchange

You have the last of the dark eyes
that could burn a borer from an ear of corn.
Eyes since are merely blue or brown,
but in your high, hard cheeks I can see
the look my mother and I both carry on.
Fretting, you lie beneath my hands,

much the same way you lay upstairs,
one spring day, and bore my blue mother,
and watched her chest begin to heave,
while outside your window a bluebird
landed on the wire. You always remember
the bird. There's no Heaven, no Hell,

you say, hoping, I suppose, that I'll argue
for salvation, resurrection, for the old ones
to rise again in their heavy shoes. I wield
soap and balm, and pray only that I live
to be old, giving you my touch not in exchange
for any softness, and not for five dollars pay

from your shoe box, but because, like you,
I'm stubborn and proud. I forget your betrayals
of my mother: trimming her long hair to her ears—
pretending a foot was an inch, telling others
her secrets, baring your cold, hard truths
until she flew into view of my father who turned

his physicist's mind to sonnets and won her.
Who might she have been without you? But then,
who am I without memory—your yellow cat
curled in sleep around my feet, you in a nightie
stirring oatmeal at the iron stove while the smell
of violets drifts from your powdered breasts. Heal.

Throw on your clothes. Put on your rouge.
Bang out into another year of mornings, fog,
falling leaves, snow—always ready for that flash of blue,
and I'll make up your bed and go.

Kissing the Sky

The year the passion plant bloomed
my boy was fifteen—safety pins piercing
his ears, eyes lined with kohl,
and hair cut in a Mohawk like the shock
of black hair he was born with.
                        Blossoms
filled the kitchen window of the insane house
where his new step-father and I
hissed at each other like crowded cats,
while my son sealed himself in his smoky room
and kissed the sky with Jimi Hendrix
whom he'd first heard in utero.
                        The plant,
grown from a cutting ten years before,
blossomed only the year we lived there,
forced by our fierceness, wood heat, and wide
south windows—flowering for my punk son,
proving that a vine remembers where it's from,
as its finger-like petals uncurl from the hard, tight buds.

In the Lingerie Store

They're enough to make anyone want
a restless body, flawless skin, and a hint
of flowers between the legs, these films
the color of evening clouds, and silk cups
with slivered bones, thin as a baby's ribs.
But in the dressing room, when I wrestle
out of heavy clothes and stand, exposed
before the mirror, fear turns me around
to check for hidden cameras, because
my breasts that rode happily all day
now lie there sleepy and blue-veined
in the thin light and refuse to fit these
frail contraptions.
                    Outside, it's dusk.
The sky is the deep blue of a slip I admired;
a half moon reclines above the roof tops.
Here, I can imagine again you watching
as I undress each night. Oh, and I remember
how once my engorged breasts felt like bombs,
tight and intricately mapped with veins,
the ducts swollen like juice sacs
inside an orange, how I could spray a stream
across the room, and how my infant son
flashed his eyes at me, bit down, and finally
sucked as though his life depended on it.

III

A Nurse Reads *A Book of Luminous Things*

She picks it up in stray moments,
one poem while the water boils,
but on duty the book stays in her bag,
hidden and reassuring as her working heart.

At the moment, the towel dispenser
enrages her as it emits one inadequate
square of rough paper—seconds she doesn't
have—there are pills to give,

catheters and dressings to change,
and Mabel is sitting in her doorway crying
forever, "I'm so afraid, where am I?"
because the line from her mind to her throat

is broken, and touch, hot coffee,
a shawl and Xanax haven't helped.
Outside the open windows, evening
is lavender light and the scent of lilacs,

summer rising from earth's body,
the air ripe and shimmering.
Inside, the call bells ring, a sound
that pierces like a needle along a hem.

"Jesus," the nurse says quietly, unable
to imagine past 11:15 when she'll leave.
Up the hallway comes Joe in his wheelchair,
his feet walking as he wheels, lost inside

Alzheimer's incessant motion.
He pauses at the desk,
holds up a calendar for her, and says,
clearly, loudly, "June!"

and smiles so fully she can see the letters
click into place in his brain,
where the word is opening a road
lined with trees bent beneath the weight

of purple blossoms, and he is driving slowly,
the radio on, and his true love,
who's a very young woman, sits neatly
beside him when anything is possible.

Black Ice

We come onto the ice like bears
dressed in wool against the wind—
and when we see the naked forms
of turtles roaming the pond bottom
with their big plates of diamonds
and squares catching the last yellow sun,
we begin to glide on our skates,
trailing our frozen breath and shadows
over the dark shapes below
as we orbit and spin in reply
to their slow movements. How we must
loom like trees, as if our feet
were leaping into their layer of the world
where we'll find what we've lost
and what we haven't become.
Snow is in the air. Soon, the ice
will grow between us, white and blind.

The Waiting

When I played Old Maid, my great aunts
were what fell to me with the losing card:
hairnets, brooches, cotton stockings,

and lessons. One does not show ones knees
or panties, one saves everything. But now,
it's as though they were never here, my aunts

who left and moved out of life with my childhood
shut in their fat black purses, leaving me
a bed and linens, a collection of thread.

Now, I'm trying to go back to the table
where eighty-pound Mida served up turkey
and admonitions, her small body a vessel

for words that slapped my hands off the table
in that cramped dining room, dark as church,
where my mother, in pearls, passed cut glass

bowls of cranberries and pickles to my quiet father.
Corrine, soft and bosomy, and thin Mida would pop up
simultaneously to fill dishes, as if they'd spent

their lives together practicing for this. We ate
and ate as November light lowered into the trees,
until the white linen and silver grew dull,

and I was excused to the living room
with my brothers and the afternoon sun.
While the grownups drank coffee from thin cups

we played with the only toy, a wooden pin dish
with a magnet-beaked bird perched on a spring,
and we lay on the rug, bad, modern children,

snapping the spring so hard the bird went wild
and spilled pins on the floor. I grew hot and tired
waiting, and found myself drifting further
and further away beneath the slow-ticking clock.

She Steps Closer

Every day she steps closer to the place
her mother has gone to. Gone
with the ruby goblets and the diamond
window above the hallway stairs.
"I feel as though I'm trapped," she says,
and I know the shrinking steps
she'll take from toilet to chair. Soon
the sun will rise and set around her bed.
We'll scatter her covers with seeds
and old bread, and open her windows to the birds.

Climbing Grief

High above the daughters' cries
and awful talk of who gets
the silver and dining room set,
cicadas buzz in the heat of July
on this cliff that looks down on
the blue lake fingered like an amoeba.
Barks of dogs on cottage lawns
and the hum of a boat cutting wake
blow upward from a former world.
A hawk floats on the wind below
looking for the smallest motion.

    At the end she left cake uncovered
    on her counter for the mice.

Here on wide ledges, on the hips
and shoulders of her world,
juniper and wild blueberries
soften the skeletal mountain
that wind and glaciers scraped bare.

    She showed bones we'd never seen
    inside the heavy fruit of her body.

Within the baking scent of a red pine,
with last year's needles scattered like fur
and new ones radiating from each branch,
a wood thrush spills its morning song
like water, like her beads falling into a dish.

    She didn't mention love, but told us
    of flocks of finches and warblers
    rising from the back fields of her childhood,
    flocks which we've only seen
    the size of in starlings.

Sound asserts itself here in flies
and bumblebees, in the castanetted flight
of grasshoppers flinging themselves
from one hot rock to another,
while wind climbs from leaf to leaf
up rising miles of mountain.

In the end
she walked barefoot each morning,
leaning her weight against table and stove,
making her way to the cupboard
to see how much the mice had eaten.

The Strip

Outside Walmart, above rows of vans and sedans
and islands of small, matching trees, above
power lines and the flat roofs of Shop N' Save,
Minute Car Wash and VIP, the sun sets
like a wheel, sending salmon-colored spokes
across ice-green one hundred and eighty degrees
from horizon to lost horizon. Shopping carts
rattle by. A mother slaps with her voice;
her toddler wails and cries. Car doors slam.
Exhaust rises like gauze; mirrors catch fire.
The Salvation Army bell keeps ringing, ringing.
One woman across the street remembers a pasture
where Holsteins grazed and lowed under elms,
how one bare December day the cows broke
barbed wire, and trampled scrub to the shore
where she and her father finally found them
painted by setting sun, lost and mooing
with tight udders. She wasn't sorry to see
it all go. She'd seen cows and trees all her life.
It thrilled her to walk the aisles in her stack heels
past rows of blenders, TVs, greeting cards
and underwear that shouldn't be used, even to dust.
Did she imagine so much pavement, the ocean
glinting between strip malls, the jays' cries
muffled by engines and horns, or the way the sun,
blind and burning, would turn through the sky
each day and lay color as if it were needed?

Sight Distance

Standing at the blackboard, the engineer explains
the hill's cross-section, the proposed straight-shot
once the peak is dynamited. He speaks of the distance
you can identify an object from a car window as if
spotting a skunk two hundred feet away compares

to knowing the moment you'll die. He says this road
was once dirt—never *really* designed (but don't we all
come from dust, lead intricate lives, and then return?)—
that sugar maples stand where he's planned ditches

(trees, a hundred years old). He says you can't stop
progress. So in three weeks, instead of maples,
there'll be only absence, and you'll read in *Science*
how biologists have proven trees' cells expand
and contract with the tides (which is not so different

from the way we cycle with the pulling moon).
He says *he* loves trees too, but a road is a road.
And he glistens as he expounds, a man who's spent
his life designing grade and incline, because he

believes in this, and can imagine the smooth macadam
shimmering on a hot day—its crisp white shoulder lines,
center stripes sharp as goldenrod—stretching for miles
as it races and curves through fields and towns—as if
it were a sea-going river, as if it were beautiful.

Eighty-Five

"Shoo," she says and waves me away
like a big fly, though she's been happy to talk,
her lipsticked mouth taking me word by word
through her life: born in this town, never left,
widowed once, divorced twice, one daughter—
now dead—and forty years in the fish factory.

She and the girls loved every minute of it,
racing—piece work, you know. Gossip swooping
through the long room like a flock of starlings
while their hands, separate animals, filled
hundreds of tins day after day. Some days
they'd lift a big icy fish from the crate,

lay it on the boiler to steam, then eat it
with their fingers. There was never anything
so fresh. She fiddles with a button on her robe,
her nails roughly painted to match her mouth,
and, no, *she* doesn't need help with her shampoo,
washing her creases, soaking her swollen feet.

She looks as though she never could get out
of that chair, but somehow it's easy
to see how she would have stood on a corner
in the South End, her feet in pumps, one hip
cocked, talking to a girlfriend, and seeming
not to notice the men from the shipyard loose
on a Saturday night in their clean white shirts.

Snow

The old, blue-eyed woman in the bed
is calling down snow. Her heart is failing,
and her eyes are two birds in a pale sky.
Through the window she can see a tree

twinkling with lights on the banking
beyond the parking lot. Lawns are still green
from unseasonable weather. Snow
will put things right; and, sure enough,

by four darkness carries in the first flakes.
Chatter, hall lights, and the rattle of walkers
spill through her doorway as she lies there—
ten miles (half a world) of ocean

between her and her home island.
She looks out from a bed the size of a dinghy.
Beyond the lit tree, beyond town, open water
accepts snow silently and, farther out,

the woods behind her house receive the snow
with a faint ticking of flakes striking needles
and dry leaves—a sound you would not believe
unless you've held your breath and heard it.

Coming Home

Oh, God, the full-faced moon is smiling at me
in his pink sky, and I'm alive, alive(!)
and driving home to you and our new refrigerator.
A skin of snow shines on the mountain beyond Burger King
and this garden of wires and poles and lighted signs.
Oh, I want to be new, I want to be the girl I saw
last night at the mike, sex leaking from her fingertips
as they traveled down to pick at her hem.
She was younger than I've ever been, with hair cropped,
ragged clothes, and face as clear as a child's.
She read as though she were in bed, eyes half closed,
teeth glistening, her shimmering body written
beneath her dress. She held every man in the audience
taut, and I thought of you. Now I'm coming home
dressed in my sensible coat and shoes, my purse
and a bundle of groceries beside me. When I arrive
we'll open the door of our Frigidaire
to its shining white interior, fill the butter's
little box, set eggs in their hollows, slip meats
and greens into separate drawers, and pause
in the newness of the refrigerator's light
while beside us, through the window,
the moon will lay a sheet on the kitchen floor.

IV

Ida Goes to the Hens

When all the day had fallen down
and the moon floated up, pale as a soul,
she left the house, each dish in its
place, left her shell in the still-made
bed and went out to sleep with the hens.

Inside their shed that was hung with dusk
and webs, the birds roosted in a row,
eyes closed, heads tucked to heated breasts.
They didn't seem to mind an old woman
settling in the midst of them. When she

wobbled, kneeling in midair, her feet
too big for the roost, the hens
on either side cozied in to hold her
with their feathered breathing until
they dreamed they flew to the tops of trees,

dreamed of free rein in the garden,
sweet greens and grubs, warm,
ripe tomatoes on the vine, rows
of tiny, graduated eggs in line to be
born, a clutch like cobblestones,

belly-warmed. And that stirring
of beak on shell. The rhythm of each day
falling into the lap of the next.
The hens did not wake when rats
crept in to feed. Ida crouched in fear,

watching the sneaking forms below,
the sparks of eyes, the hairless tails.
The nudging birds whispered, "sleep,
sleep," until she grew soft as down
and slept to the sound of teeth in grain

while the full-yolk moon pulled them hour
by hour to dawn until the rooster
ruffled his chest and cascading tail,
stretched his luminous throat and
crowed another sun up from behind the hills.

The murmuring hens fluffed and flurried
to the straw to lay. They filled the house
with triumphant cackling. Ida,
hearing this as hymns, reached out
her ready hand to fill

her apron pockets with still-warm eggs.

October

Into the tail-feathered sumac
all light is absorbed
except for red

which crows its color
as the bird that wakes us
throws morning

from his throat
while he struts his plumage
among the leafy hens.

Leaving Her Body

When she died I held on
while her ragged breath stopped
and she became as still
as a porcupine lying in the road.
I waited for the sigh
of her spirit leaving her body
the way she'd felt her own mother
flash by like a bird. I felt
nothing but absence.
She'd said none of us believe
we'll ever have to
leave this garden. But summer
has turned belly-up
to a hard frost. Squash vines rust.
Monarchs disappear.
The chill is more than weather
can account for.

Love and Pain

After the funeral there is, of course,
the big house, good food, an expansive
view of the bay and a small book for writing
memories—how could I not remember,

surrounded by former family, the past
reeling its old home-movie, jerking
from scene to scene, shots of love
and pain caught holding each other?

Ruth, I was the one who stood by
as you did your son's wash, held up
a sheet and said, "He gets these stains,"
and we both knew they weren't sweat

or tears, but neither of us had language
to go further and prevent what came.
And I was the girl who lay in his arms,
upstairs in your small green house,

believing that when our bodies died,
our love, trailing a tail of light,
would rocket to the stars—and then your car
drove in and your son leapt off me,

pulled on T-shirt and jeans, swung
his skinny legs out the window, and
appeared moments later at your door.
Now, in his house, you're gone; I walk

from room to room, kiss his wife, kiss
our son, kiss former in-law after in-law,
and kiss him. Grief drapes the lawn
where his younger children swing,

curls inside his jacket buttons,
tucks beneath the crackers and cheese,
and it rides in my throat, sneaking up
from the deepest pockets of my body

like TB waking after a long sleep. "I'll be
careful what I write in that book," I tell him,
and he laughs, throwing his head back
so that his palate shows, and for a moment,

it's as if that pink flesh, riding inside
its shell of bone and teeth, were his soul.

After a Dark Winter

Medium is best, the two friends agree,
having talked their way down to the core
of friendship, the conversation moved
by red wine rich as a carpet. Penises,

of course, are what they're discussing,
two women lucky enough to have indulged
in the days before sex could kill them.
They agree that big is too big.

Through a dinner of lamb and baby greens
they talk about fat, brains, money and food,
then swallow the last sip and step out
into evening. At eight the sky is pale silk.
Music and laughter erupt from outdoor cafes

jammed with people and the odors
of steaks and sauces. At one round table
a man and woman lean over plates, the power
of love or ovulation or electromagnetism
pulling their faces together. The two women

sigh, but walk on and buy sundaes.
One tells the other a dream where a beautiful,
dark-haired man looked into her eyes.
There was no world beyond the bed, no language

except skin. They moved as water moves,
and when she kissed him, his mouth
was filled with bittersweet chocolate. Ohhh,
the friends want *that*, now, the one who has
love, and the other who has money.

And do they both want what the other has,
or at least a kind of diffusion, so they can taste
each other's lives the way they shared
hors d'oeuvres the night before?
They head home down Newbury Street

which is lit, its glittering shops
displaying dresses and couches, platters,
jewels and shoes, window after window
of goods wanting to be entered,
waiting to enter real lives.

The Muse Visits After I'll Never Write Another Chicken Poem

You arrive, and I become the white hen
that is taking her first spring bath

in the south-wall garden which warms
early. Legs thrashing and wings

scrambling the dirt to a fine dust,
she works earth between every feather,

then flops in the sun and forgets
the rooster's talons and beak,

forgets Winter's long, dark reach,
and forgets the daily (even
this morning's) strain of the egg—for this.

Mission San Xavier Del Bac

Inside the stucco shell
where faith is pulled from wood
and plaster by a restorer's brush, shades
of blood and moss, water and cantaloupe,
yolk and ocotillo cry, "Believe, believe!"
A man kneeling before the altar converts
blank space to dizzying geometrics. Mary,
life-sized, grieved, and recessed in the east
chapel wall, is dressed in a gown of lace
and pale blue satin. Painted saints
occupy high-rise niches, but Judas
is missing from his alcove behind the pulpit
as noticeably as an absent tooth.

A man and a woman bright as paint enter
God's stage, which is roped off— the man,
a Tohono O'Odham, paunchy and strong,
who doesn't understand how, but he's
found his calling, frescoing churches—
and an Austrian, his teacher, who never
dreamed she'd leave Europe, marry an Indian
and move to the reservation.

I've forgotten why Judas betrayed Jesus,
and which angel hovers above me,
but I could take communion for all this
color, wash this couple's feet. I don't
need to know if they fight. I'm ready
to bow down and pin my griefs and prayers
to dead Father Kino's habit with the other
paper pleas and milagros, to light
a candle to the Virgin, and pray
that my calling calls me, that the world
will not end, as the natives believed,
if the cat carved over the mission door
creeps closer, and reaches the mouse.

Salvage

In the last week before Rite Aid tears down
our grandfather's house, my brother and I
go from room to dirty room and talk it back
to a time when the hallway smelled as rich
as church with its polished wood

and carpet on the stairs, when a piano sat
behind French doors, and this town's first TV
commandeered the living room. Only then
do we begin taking down four-panel doors,
prying Victorian molding from windows,

hauling porcelain sinks from the wall, saving
anything we can. Gramp's black Cadillac
sails through the kitchen, and his swan boat,
tiny now, swirls down the drain. The sad-eyed girl,
big as life in a painting, drops her white dog

and bursts into tears. A doorknob rattles,
one my brother rattled as a baby, and the tablecloth
I ruined with a knife flaps from room to room.
Overhead our father's mysterious childhood
dabbles in gunpowder and equations

while my own sits on a small step
between the bathroom floor and a locked door
with painted panes and waits for something
to happen. Soon it will—a wrecking ball
crashing through plaster walls and windows—

while my family still sits on the upstairs porch
with pie and tall glasses of milk on an afternoon
thirty years ago, not knowing that Gramp's heart
will stop the next day, not knowing we'll lose
everything here except, all these years later,

this salvage we've been granted before the dark
attics and closets and the long, sunlit rooms
converge into rubble. On our last day
my brother hacks the furnace loose and cuts
the cellar's copper pipes as though he's

some crazed and greasy surgeon gutting
bowels with his SawsAll. I stand
in the dim hallway and tear out the house's mouth,
the brass intercom plate where I once
reached above my head, pushed the buzzer,

and waited for the deep voice to sound
like God's through a blossom of holes,
waited for the click of the lock
on the plateglass door, the only thing
standing between me and that world overhead.

The Living Room

Twenty miles out you'll cross a bridge,
so low you'd have to hug your knees
to glide under in a canoe, where
the stream flows through the marsh

so slowly you see it move only
as a leaf rides the water's skin.
Up the hill, a half mile on the left,
you come to a white house, *Thelma's*

Haven of Rest. Pull into the drive,
lock your phone and keys inside the car,
walk up the steps, and knock four times,
hearing the sound travel the hall.

A woman in an apron, the poet
of chicken pie and beans, will answer
and lead you to her living room,
papered green and dark behind blinds,

where you'll sit and begin to forget,
piece by piece, the sounds of a clock
in another room, your own breath
as limpid as water, the smells of soap

and baking—everything except
Thelma's fingers, as she smooths
your tired face the way we soothe a
child, or the way we close the eyes

of the dead so that the body will not
watch and mourn as the spirit
touches each cell, gathers itself,
and leaves the adored flesh.

The Island

The sand shone with grains of silver, and waves
ran up the beach with foaming paws. Mother
undressed and we saw her heavy breasts
where we had fed as babies. Father wandered the island,
gathering driftwood for the fire, while we pulled off
our own clothes and showed our bodies, pale
as the underbellies of pollack we had caught,
slit open, and swept clean with our fingers.
The feel of our nakedness as we swam would come back
in rare dreams from which we would awaken,
the membrane of dreaming still on us.
My brother's navel was a perfect shell.
Our white boat rocked on the incoming tide.

Conception

On my forty-sixth birthday my father
wrote that he remembered my conception
in intimate detail. That's all he said.
Hoping I'd imagine the rest? I knew

some stories: sonnets he composed to woo
my mother, the time she lifted his thick
glasses and kissed his eyes, a naked swim,
snippets of life before it bore down,

before the forces that hold love shifted.
She told me once I was easy to conceive,
as if I'd been "waiting to come in."
Intriguing notion, the spirit watching,

perhaps coaxing, the sperm and egg
on their difficult journey—whispering
in her ear as she readied herself,
then appeared on the curved stair and said,

"Come here." He closed his book, rose, followed
the ample curve of her bottom which swam
before his myopic eyes, slightly out
of focus, awash in her sheer white gown

like a moon behind haze. While her fingers
unbuttoned his shirt, released his buckle,
the day's compounds and equations drifted
away. The word *baby* blew in, then out,

and my father was inside my mother,
stroking to the outer reaches. When he
washed back, he found her again, drifting
beneath him, and he moved a little to see

the sated look on her face, to admire
her breasts' quiet rise and fall. He lay there,
his breath slipping in and out, and waited.

Elizabeth Tibbetts's poems have been published in journals including *The American Scholar, The Beloit Poetry Journal, Green Mountains Review,* and *Prairie Schooner,* and have been nominated three times for the Pushcart Prize. She works as a nurse, and she and her husband live in a rural part of Maine where her family has been settled for many generations.